SPARK & FIZZ BOOKS PRESENTS

PLANET SCUMM

WINTER 2018   "O SCUMM ALL YE FAITHFUL"   ISSUE NO. 6

———— A FAITHFUL TABLE OF CONTENTS ————

EDITOR IN CHIEF	CREATIVE DIRECTOR	MANAGING EDITOR	EDITOR	ILLUSTRATIONS
SEAN CLANCY	ALYSSA ALARCÓN SANTO	TYLER BERD	ERIC LOUCKS	SAM RHEAUME

Planet Scumm is a triannual short fiction anthology. Visit **planetscumm.space** for submissions.

© SPARK & FIZZ BOOKS
Second Printing, 2019   ISBN: 978-1-970154-00-9   Portland | Boston | New York

MISSION: SCUMM

Status report, Miss... whatever your codename is this week. The Earther job. One target. Live capture. Your quarry is an... entertainer of sorts. Broadcasts over any wavelength it can wrap its slimy little pseudobrain around. There was one more detail too... Ah, yes, here it is. It flies around on a PLANET-SIZED SPACESHIP!

And you still haven't found it.

I've been your handler for a few cycles now, Miss. If my species was capable of empathy I'd say we've grown... close. Since that isn't the case, however, I'll say this: those Earther idiots are dropping mad spacebucks to catch this Scummy sonofabitch. If we don't get him, some other shadowy, jacked-up paramilitary outfit will. So make with the spy stuff, okay?

Oh, and make sure you file your travel expenses before the end of the week.

Trail's gone cold, Z3B. Not a trace. I've been to every weapons stockpile and novelty gag shop on this side of the system, and all I have to show for it is this peculiar rubberized noise cushion.

Anyway—seems nobody has seen our target. Found another Earther by the name of j.l. oneill. Thought he might have hitched a ride off his ill-fated planet before Scummy blew it to hell. No such luck. Earther said he got halfway across the galaxy by traveling through a payphone, if you can believe it. Had a whole set of instructions typed up—I've saved a copy on our systems if you're interested, filed under *"Touch-tone."*

Hologram vendors are making the rounds again with this season's latest models. I figure the only way our target could hide a spaceship as big as his is with some sort of stealth field. I staked out that *"Muttonscalp"* holo-museum with

I. Horsburgh, hoping our goo-man would show up. He didn't, but I did see this really inspiring exhibit on death by exposure. Gave me some great ideas for when we get back in the assassination game.

Remember that folk tale we caught wind of back in the last system? Come on, you remember—Hailey Piper told it the whole department when we checked in at the office. People skinned alive by some kind of creeping, crawling monster. Yeah, "Scarlet Hide Molly," that's the one! Doesn't have anything to do with our catching Scummy—I just thought it was cool as hell. Wish we were chasing ol' Scarlet Hide instead of this snotty little creep.

This job's getting me down, I tell ya. I was trading stories with the owner at the refueling station--Klaus Wenzel, if memory serves. Told him I track and kill sentient beings for a living. He told me that at his last job you had to face down a portal of infinite, eldritch energy if you wanted to make upper management. Said that's what it took to be "The Company Man." Seemed like he was trying to one-up me, but damn if it wasn't a good story.

You been following the reports about the Gl'iel, Z3B? Seems there isn't a planet they won't try to take over. Have to give it to them, though—they're expert infiltrators. Looks like they may have even made a move for Earth before the whole Scummy incident. James Dorr—he's the guy in our Analytics Department—ran a simulation on possible strategies. Turns out the Gl'iel look similar to some Earther festival creature called an "elf." Anyway, I've got it under "Holly Jolly" if you want to- hey! Wait, Z3B! Don't sit on that cushion! Well of course it makes a great fart noise, but it's also full of nerve toxin.

O SCUMM ALL YE FAITHFUL!

Spark & Fizz Books 2018
Portland | Boston | New York

AUTHORS

J.L.ONEILL is a Hamilton-based writer, poet, and apprentice electrician whose work can be found right here inside this magazine you're reading and *The WiFiles*. He co-wrote the short film *The Freelancer* for the Hamilton 24-Hour Film Festival, which placed in the top 10. He has graduated from Mohawk College twice—he first time in Electrical Engineering and the second in Writing for Publication. Currently he is working towards his B.A. in English at York University. Follow him on instagram @jl.oneill before it's too late.

ISOBEL HORSBURGH lives on South Tyneside in North East England. She used to be a longterm carer and currently works in the library at the University of Northumbria. Her work has appeared in *SPACESQUID, PHOBOS, GATHERING STORM, STRANGE BEASTIES, NOIR: AT THE SALAD BAR, IT'S ALL TRUMPED UP* and *SECRET STAIRS*.

HAILEY PIPER was born obsessed with monsters, ghosts, and all things that go bump in the night. Today she puts her Bachelor's degree in Literature to use writing horror stories to feed that obsession. When reading, she's either hopping between three short story anthologies simultaneously across several weeks or devouring a novel in a weekend, no middle ground. A good day can't be great without a trip to the library, because she is a nerd and loving it. She and her wife live in the D.C. metro area.

KLAUS WENZEL, intergalactic reporter, travels the farthest reaches of the universe to collect precious oddities in the name of *PLANET SCUMM*. His ship's crew consists of a brilliant Italian knockout, three English-speaking cats, and an old dog who enjoys swimming in zero gravity.

JAMES DORR's latest book is a novel-in-stories, *TOMBS: A CHRONICLE OF LATTER-DAY TIMES OF EARTH*, published in June 2017 by Elder Signs Press. Working mostly in dark fantasy/horror with some forays into science fiction and mystery, his *THE TEARS OF ISIS* was a 2013 Bram Stoker Award® finalist for Superior Achievement in a Fiction Collection, while other books include *STRANGE MISTRESSES: TALES OF WONDER AND ROMANCE, DARKER LOVES: TALES OF MYSTERY AND REGRET*, and his all-poetry *VAMPS (A RETROSPECTIVE)*. He has also been a technical writer, an editor on a regional magazine, a full time non-fiction freelancer, and a semi-professional musician, and currently harbors a Goth cat named Triana. An Active Member of SFWA and HWA, Dorr invites readers to visit his blog at jamesdorrwriter.wordpress.com.

J.L. ONEILL

TOUCH-TONE

Listen here: You don't want to try this.

I'm sure you know—it is the reason you are reading this, after all—scientists in a secret subterranean facility within the Gobi Desert found a way to travel to another dimension. Otherworld, they call it. Where and what Otherworld is remains unknown. However, opening the gateway is as simple as dialing a phone number.

Before You Begin

The Otherworld is similar to ours in the sense that basic physics still apply.

Similar does not mean the same. What I mean to say is there are new rules, new laws of science and nature, that we do not have the capacity to understand. The crucial difference between here and there are the grim un-beings that inhabit Otherworld. They possess the power to strip the flesh and soul from your body with the violence of a Siberian hailstorm. Never acknowledge their presence. Ever. Those who deviate from this step by step guide never return. Decide who you are. Decide to follow the path.

The jump from our world to Otherworld can only be attempted

during the shortest day of the year, at the darkest hour, when the sun is farthest from the horizon. December 21st between 12:13 and 12:31 in the morning. Eighteen minutes. Eighteen minutes to open the gateway to the Otherworld. It is of grave importance that the night is clear. If it is not—f there is even a slight wind, or chance of snowfall or rain––do not attempt this. You will not return.

The items you will need, according to the Canadian Zero Division agents who leaked the original email to NATO, are as follows:

Warm clothes—sweater, shirt, long johns, jacket, thermal socks, boots, gloves––that can withstand at least -30 degrees Celsius weather, a military grade flashlight with a wrist strap, a touch-tone payphone, two dollars in change—to use said phone—a cellular phone, and a death wish.

Cellphone and landline signals are not strong enough to open the gateway to Otherworld. The phone must be a hardline and outside, in frigid elements. We do not know why. This may require you to open the gateway in public, outside a gas station or beside a con-venience store in a shitty part of town. Choose one under, or adjacent to, an operational streetlight. If you do not, you risk missing the opening of the gateway, which could result in a false sense of security. You could be lost forever with the hoarfrost-coated bodies of UN troops and other idiotic thrill seekers and failed pathfinders such as yourself.

This is your last warning. Do not attempt this.

Instructions

Attach the flashlight dongle to your wrist. You do not want to be found alone in the dark without it. Make it tight. Tighter. Good.

The last thing you need to know is: Never. Hang. Up. The. Phone. If you wish to leave at any moment dial the voicemail on your cellphone and enter # # # 3 6 7 4 4 8 3 1 6 3 *. The gateway will close. You will be safe. You can go home. Do not make another attempt to open the gate. They will remember you.

Insert the required amount of change to make a call. Dial the following sequence into the touchtone phone between 12:13 and 12:31 in the morning:

* 2 4 4 5 3 7 3 6 1

Wait until the operator's voice asks you to complete the call by entering a valid phone number.

After the third prompt enter:

6 3 1

An invalid number message will play. Do not hang up. Do not try your call again. Wait until the machine swallows your money. Insert enough change to make another call. A brown station wagon will drive past you. The blue glow from its high beams will scratch at your eyes like dry ice and make them water. This is supposed to happen. Wipe your tears away before they freeze.

Enter the following combination into the phone:

8 4 3 3 2 6 6 3 3

The streetlight should go out. The steady mechanical hum of the dial tone will continue coming through the receiver and sink into the frozen world around you. The streetlight should come on again. If it does not, pull out your cellphone immediately, call your voicemail, and dial the extraction number. They were waiting for you. You must leave. If you hear anything on your cellphone—heavy breathing, violent screams, a child crying, insectoid chittering, even your own voice, friendly or malevolent—do not listen to it. It is not you. It cannot be you. Resist the insidious sounds. Dial the exit number. Never attempt opening the gateway again. They will always be waiting for you.

If the streetlight comes back on, a low mist will fill the darkness around you and wash the frozen world in a numb, greyscale haze. The illumination from the streetlight will flicker, fizzle, and explode like shattered icicles. Stay calm. This is normal.

Enter:

1 4 1 2 3 4 1 9 6 8

The operator will ask you to re-enter the last number. It is a trick. Do not re-enter. Wait. She will ask you again. Wait. She will say your name and ask you politely to enter the last digit. Do not respond. When she threatens you, pull out your cellphone and dial your voicemail. She will be on the other line. Listen to her banshee screams echo as she threatens you and your loved ones. She will promise to mutilate them while you watch if you do not answer her. Do not answer her. Do not hang up. Do not put your cellphone down. It is your only way back to our world.

Dial the following into the touchtone phone:

1 6 7 3 6 1

The brown car will drive past again. Its headlights will be off this time. It is imperative you do not watch it drive past you. If the driver calls out to you for directions, or to help repair his car, ignore him. He is one of them. He is an un-being. He may leave his car and his gelatinous mass will approach you, sluggishly dragging over the tarmac in sticky thwacks. You must not look at him. Do not respond. Do not clear your throat. Do not shrug. For God's sake, do not turn your back to him. Just ignore him. He will

J.L.ONEILL

become irritated and retreat into the fog, silently watching as you continue your call.

When he leaves, dial:

9

Footsteps will approach you from behind. Do not look for the source. If you wish to leave, you have approximately 20 seconds to decide and enter the exit number into your cellphone, after which the footsteps will hasten, clicking and clacking on the concrete. They will stop. She will be behind you. Watching you. Do not turn around.

When her footfalls cease dial:

6 8 7

She will try to get your attention, but you must not respond. She is the woman from the phone. The one who threatened to mutilate you and your loved ones, the one who said she would find you. She has.

Dial: 1

She will ask you a series of questions in a calm, almost loving voice. How long you are going to be, can you stay with her until she finishes her call (because it is awfully scary out tonight), what are you doing out this late, are you alone, do you feel alone sometimes, where is everyone, are you shy or something, why can't you speak? She will demand eye contact, call

you rude, or handsome, or beautiful. Do not respond. Do not make a sound. Not a cough, or a sigh, or a nervous laugh. The un-being behind you feeds off sound. She does not have a face and you must not look at it. Underneath her long hair is an empty shell where light dies.

When she mentions the weather, dial:

4 2

The Otherworld will grow cold. Snow will fall from unseen clouds in the endless darkness above you. It will float in delicate wisps at first, but soon the wind will roar and swirl around you with the violence of a cyclone, raking frozen chunks of snow against your body. If you do not act quickly, the current will carry you away from the touch-tone phone. You can try to find the pay phone in the blizzard, guided by your flashlight—if you did not lose it. Or, you could risk dialing the exit number into your cellphone before she or the gelatinous man find you. Before the wind rips your cellphone from your frostbitten fingers.

Dial: 8

The woman will creep forward, her faceless head tilted as she watches you with deep primordial eyes. She will stand beside you, may even place her pale, corpse-cold hand on your shoulder, or slip it under your toque to brush her skeletal fingers through your hair. You must use your peripherals to watch her. Focus on anything but her. Resist the urge to hang up and run. She will catch you. She always does. Check the color of her jacket. It should be red. If it is any other colour dial the exit number into your cellphone. She will lash out like a rabid polar bear and rip the touch-tone phone from the ground while you dial for safety. You must not run. You must stand sure and complete the sequence. If you enter the wrong digit, she will kill you. If she is wearing a red coat, dial:

3 9 2 9

She will scream. It will sound both guttural and ear-splitting, like a Kodiak mauling a piglet.

As she calls other un-beings to help peel the flesh from your bones, press: *

If you entered everything correctly, she will disappear. The snow will float peacefully to the ground. You do not want to know what happens if you dialed wrong.

The return number has changed. You may leave the touch-tone phone and wander Otherworld, or come back to us. The choice is yours.

To return home dial:

4 6 3 0 2 3 0 9 4 8 4 0 9 3 *

You are free to explore the icy wastelands of Otherworld. Un-beings lurking in frozen shadows will see you, but they cannot hurt you. Although the batteries in your electronics will never die, do not take a photo of yourself. If you see your reflection without the proper filter you will claw at your face and stomach to free yourself from the confines of the construct you are using to explore this glacial wasteland.

In the ruins of a forlorn city, between rotting brick and mortar, hide other humans seeking shelter. They came to Otherworld the same way you did, but lost their way. Pay them no mind. They are lost now.

In the snow dunes to the east is a tribe of pale fox-mouse creatures we assume were the food source of the un-beings until humans arrived. There are snow-capped mountains of glassed ice standing sentinel in the south, over-shadowing a flotilla of white icebergs and frozen fjords. An endless lake is to the north. There is nothing to the west. Nothing.

An hour in Otherworld could be anywhere from one minute to eight days our time. The length of your stay is based on your stomach. No edible foods grow in the frostbitten tundra. Few claim to have seen any. Those who did recalled a berry made from spun glass, which shone deep blue. They ate it to prolong their stay. Shortly after their return, their organs shut down as they froze to death from the inside out.

I do not mean to worry you. I mean for you to return.

Come back to us whenever you feel the need. The number, again, is:

4 6 3 0 2 3 0 9 4 8 4 0 9 3 *

Do not be alarmed when you enter it. The voice sounds like rancid seal meat ripped through demon jowls. "There are no gods here." Rejoice. It means you've returned. You're home.

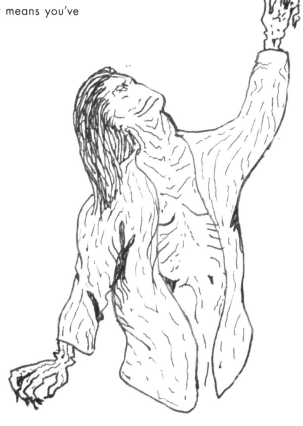

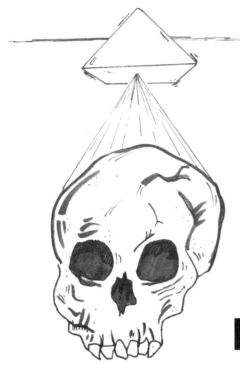

I. HORSBURGH

MUTTONSCALP

There was a soft thump at the front door. Lia raised her head from the heap of photos spread out on the polished tabletop. She didn't move from the chair. Beyond the glass, soft flakes wafted down. If they couldn't reach the bell, it was probably kids. She picked out another of the sepia photos from the file, held it up, considering. The noise came again, a single thud on the wood.

"Get lost," she thought, "I'm working." It came again, muffled but determined. "If your knuckles are bleeding, don't come crying to me."

She got to her feet, and made her way in an unhurried fashion across the hall, which had a pleasing scent of fresh paint and sawdust.

The light and airy feel in here was a big improvement on what they'd found when the house was first unlocked. It was unrecognisable, the old stone building with dripping mould on the walls, a stench of rot and a roof like moth-eaten lace. All was now scoured clean and made sound. This had been, among other things, a farmhouse, including an inn, a meeting house for non-conformists, a school, an amateur knocking-shop and a scrapyard/piggery.

It was one of those double-fronted flat-faced sandstone buildings that one saw all over the North, with Georgian windows set into in an older facade. Often marooned by a dual carriageway or on the fringe of a housing estate, stripped to the bone as nature and vandals took turns, sometimes all that was left was a collapsing husk. In this case they'd got there in time, before the whole lot toppled to the ground like an elephant with a dart in its flank. Its official name had been Muttonscalp Farm, but since a family named Winter had spent a short time living there about one hundred and fifty years ago, it was now Winter House. The Winter Trust had appointed Lia to run things. She was already known among her colleagues as the Sno Queen.

She flung open the front door, prepared to give someone an earful. There was nobody in sight, no prints on the crisp carpet at her feet. If anything had been thrown at the door from over the fence, there was no sign of it. How had they managed that?

"Bloody kids!"

Children from the housing estate had been hanging about when the contractors were working, peering through the iron gates. There was a high fence at the front, high brick walls at the back,

but they must have found a way of getting through. Winter House was for the community, of course, and there would be outreach, but Lia didn't want just anybody barging in, not yet. They were not due to open for a month or so, probably the end of June. If this was going to be the cultural hub that had been promised, you couldn't be having unauthorised snowball fights all over the place. Event management would be seeing to those, later, once there was accident insurance in place.

The Sno had set to a powdery texture that looked a lot like the real thing, as far as she knew. At the age of twenty-eight, she was too young to have ever seen real snow. They were still working on the squeak people said you could hear when it compacted underfoot. The tang in your nose, and frozen breath-- they were working on that, too.

The Sno was really coming down now, not that there was any chance of being Sno-ed in. The particles could be shifted quite easily with a big plastic scoop. It was more like being in a giant snow globe, the Snoflakes endlessly circulating. She went to take a reading from the machine, which sat unobtrusively at the base of a wall in the back garden.

As Lia stepped back inside the front door, she saw a movement at the end of the hall. A woman in a long printed-cotton dress, sprigged with blue

8

flowers, was walking past the foot of the stairs, carrying a baby in her arms. Her brown hair hung down like the ears of a spaniel. She turned her back towards Lia and walked steadily along the narrow passage towards the kitchen.

This was Martha Wake. She had died in 1838. The baby, wrapped in a shawl and pressed against her shoulder, had no face yet. There was little point in providing one. It could have been any one of her eight known children, half of whom had lived to grow up. She would have been thought lucky for that.

In the right conditions, a skull in the ground could be copied in three dimensions without excavation, and a reconstruction made. You could now see the faces of ancestors who'd never heard of cameras, the wealthier, well-nourished ones, anyway. If they had good strong bones and a marked grave, they could be brought back. If, however, your rickets-stricken forebears were bundled into a pauper's grave with a dozen strangers, you were going to have to go on using your imagination.

The faces of children were not recreated, for the same reason that there are no child crash test dummies. The tables that gave the average thickness of skin on a human skull were based on donated bodies, and parents didn't donate their children for this sort of research. Lia knew some archaeologists had disliked excavating children's graves anyway. She wouldn't call herself sentimental, but she could see their point.

In Martha's case, she'd died relatively young. There were no females of a similar age in the grave, and she had lived for a time at Muttonscalp as a servant, so she was ideal as a subject. There were others as well, a good sample of the many who'd come and gone here over the centuries. They were on shuffle, so you never knew which one you'd come across as you went about the rooms. There'd be the flick of a frock coat round a corner, the top of a bewigged head passing below as you glanced over the banister. They did not make eye contact. During tests this had been found to be a bit too unsettling for some people. They looked over your shoulder or at the ground. They moved across your path or away from you, but never towards you. Dogs didn't like them. Visitors with guide-dogs would have to be warned about that. Cats trotted through them, unfazed.

In theory, accurate voices could also have been created, but again, in tests, the voices of actors were found to be more effective. The reconstructed voices, using the bones of the neck and thorax, were croaky and at the same time, a bit too real for comfort. The first time the real Richard III spoke, he was said to have sounded like a ventriloquist's dummy with a frog trapped inside it, but technology had moved on. The Winter House 'grams were intended to maintain a dignified silence.

Lia returned to her pictures. The south-facing light of what had been the parlour was usually easy to work by if you were picking out tiny details in photographs. There was one in particular she thought would look good blown up for exhibition, Edwardian skaters on a pond, muffled up against the cold. It wasn't a Christmas card-pretty scene, the clothes were practical, but she wished she could have seen it in colour. Every so often, as she worked, a 'gram went past the door of the room. They didn't come in--this was not a public area. The 'grams circulated as long as there was somebody in the house, the motion-sensors being part of the renovation. Lia was not disturbed by them. They were only shadows, like a zoetrope. There were to be no artefacts to give a "period' feel to the house. There were museums in the region stuffed with authentic bygones, but this was not a museum, it was a gallery with exhibition spaces. The Sno outside the window was coming down so thickly, she went outside to take another reading. Again, the screen told her that all was well.

🖫

She'd listened to all the recordings in the archive, including a very old woman who could remember trying to make a snowman.

"It was all wet and slushy, and we couldn't get it to cling together. It stuck in frozen pills to our mittens. My gran could remember sledging on the Town Moor in Newcastle, on real, soft snow. She said it was like flying."

Lia tried to picture it—the ringing voices of the children in the bitter air, the fading light of a winter's afternoon long ago, the blue metal of the toboggan hitting the frozen crystals--but it was too remote.

"Starved with cold," people around here still said. But still, how must it have felt?

The Sno she had knelt in just now, while wearing knee-length shorts and a skimpy t-shirt, was warm and dry to the touch. Lia'd never worn mittens, she thought they sounded impossibly hampering. How on earth did people get anything done, dressed like that? They were going to have craft sessions at the house, knitting woollen mufflers and stockings, but what they would do with them was anyone's guess. There were rumoured to be patches of real snow in secret locations in the Highlands, but Lia reckoned you were more likely to meet the Loch Ness Monster trotting down the road

Pulling herself to her feet, she looked up at the front of the house. The falling Sno made it hard to be sure, but was that a shape crossing the mullioned window on the top floor? There was a staircase just behind it, and a landing. She couldn't see if the figure was a man or a woman, or just a cloud reflected on the pane. She knew them all: Mary Anne Haddrick, Denton Friend, Isaac Verey, Samuel Gelatly, and her favourite, Jane Codling. She'd drowned during a skating party on the frozen lake in nearby Sedgely in 1880, while the rest of the village rescued a hot chestnut machine.

This 'gram could have been any of them. Whoever had set them off should not have been in the house, though. Nobody should be. Lia took a step towards the front door, then hesitated. She should let somebody know if they had an intruder. Walking round to the back of the building, she found no footprints. The rear doors were still locked.

Back at the front, she found the hall empty. She stood just inside the door, and clapped her hands. None of the 'grams appeared. This happened sometimes. She knew they hadn't gone anywhere, although she was tempted to call for them by name, like they were mischievous children. She walked up the stone stairs, on which the real Isaac Verey had

tripped and died in 1798.

She'd read that people in the past used fire rather than lamps to light rooms, and candles were only for getting from one place to another, not always without mishap. The light in this house today was so clear, with new skylights, that it was hard to picture them stumbling about in smoky darkness. The 'grams moved with an assurance they could hardly have known in life. Nothing of their aches and pains, or ill-fitting shoes, or bare and callused feet, showed.

Upstairs, in the long gallery, blow-ups were propped against the walls, photographs of winters past. There was a woman in a sacking apron putting out scraps for birds, sheep crowding round a bale of hay, and a group of men with shovels in the terrible winter of 1947, digging an entire train out of the drifts. Birds had fallen out of the trees like stones. There would be illustrations and information panels related to the Little Ice Age, and Frost Fairs on the Thames, once they were completed.

Beyond them was something which Lia was especially proud of. The snowflakes installation hung on impossibly thin wiress. Each was the size of a dinner plate, intricate and sparkling. As the prisms of glass caught the light, rainbows were reflected on the walls and floor. If one was struck just so, it rang with music. Sometimes, when she was alone in the gallery, Lia walked through the shimmering maze of flakes, flicking them with the tip of a finger as gently as she could, so that the whole house was alive with chimes. There must have been music of some sort here once, and she would have loved to know it.

Something cold touched her shoulder for a fleeting moment, and she flinched. Putting her hand up to her collarbone, she felt dampness on her fingertips. Goosebumps rose on her bare arms. She looked up. Something had dripped from the skylight. The Sno only fell from the level of the eaves, so the glass above her was clear, but there must be condensation. She'd have to report that. No matter how meticulous the conservation, an old building will have ways of confounding you.

Walking back along the landing, she looked over the banister, expecting to see the crown of a head passing over the worn flags, but it was all stillness down there. She found a song bubbling up. Lia belonged to a choir. She'd been researching some music for them, really old songs, not familiar to most people. They hoped eventually to sell an album in the Winter House shop, along with the snowdrop mugs and the icecube fudge. They would be winter songs, not Christmassy, but something evoking the feel of

an icy cold day. The acoustics in here were perfect. She put back her head and sang.

"Under the blanket, under the snow, under the blanket of winter I'll go. Under the-" Behind her came a resounding crack, then the sound of shattered glass. If one of those snowballs had hit the window...

Running back into the gallery, it was difficult now to see clearly. Somehow Sno was covering much of the skylight! That shouldn't happen. The Sno that fell down from the eaves couldn't go upwards, even on a breezy day. Turning on the lights, she saw one of the snowflakes shattered on the wooden floor.

"I wasn't singing that high, was I?" Then she saw the snapped wire. That was going to have to be reported, they couldn't risk it happening when the visitors were in. She walked back along the landing, which was still empty of 'grams. There was a corridor stretching along the front of the building, leading to a storeroom at the end. This was where the 'gram she had seen from outside had been walking. It was hard to see much through the window, so thick was the Sno, but somebody seemed to have dumped a black bin liner near the gate.

She opened the storeroom door, feeling pity as always for the maids whose tiny bedchamber this had once been, and from the cupboard, she collected strong gloves and a shoe box, as well as a small brush. Most of the snowflake could be rescued, if she was careful. She walked back along the corridor, along the landing and into the gallery. She'd worked in old buildings before. They all have their own settling noises, and she was only just learning the music of Winter House. She closed her eyes, and stood for a moment, listening, but the Sno seemed to block any ambient noise. She half expected, when opening her eyes, to see a retreating back or a hem whisking out of sight, but the 'grams were still not in evidence. There are always teething troubles, she told herself, better to get this ironed out before the hordes arrive.

The pieces of snowflake were still scattered on the floor of the gallery, but it was now so dark that the reflections had paled. She took out her phone. The signal was never very good in the house, for some reason, but it looked as though she had a message. She didn't recognise the number. The text blinked out even as she read:

Under the blanket, I'll waken once more, dressed all in white, I'll wait at your door

She felt a long shiver that started at the top of her head and ran down through her body. There was somebody in the house, listening. They must have heard her singing, and now they were mocking her. If it was someone she knew playing a mean joke, they'd be sorry, but running through the possibilities in her mind, she couldn't think of a single colleague or friend who would do this. She wished she could, because the alternative, the stranger hiding in the house, meant she was going to have to get out. She wasn't someone who ever backed away from trouble, and being driven out of somewhere that was her own space was infuriating.

She made her way down to the hall, deliberately not running. This was a strategic withdrawal, not flight. She didn't want to end like Isaac Verey in a heap at the bottom of the stairs.

The heavy front door was shaking as though buffeted by a strong wind. She paused, watching, clutching the banister rail. Meet it head on. They won't expect that. Make yourself do it. Three strides and she was across the hall. She reached out and grasped the handle. It stuck. She yanked at it, struggling, using all her strength, her palms slippery on the metal. Swearing to herself, she tried again, and all at once it yielded, pulling her off-balance, bringing a pile of Sno in with it, far more than the machine should have been able to produce. Then she saw that some of it was melting, watery crystals dissolving into a puddle at her feet. It couldn't do that. It came from a

laboratory. It would not melt. Beyond, in the garden, a blizzard raged, and a cold she had never known bit into her. Her teeth chattered, and she flung her arms around herself. She took a step outside and sank into a drift of icy powder that numbed her bare legs. Through the whirling flakes, she could just make out a patch of black near the gate that must be the bin-bag she'd noticed from upstairs. Measured against the distant gatepost, it

was taller than she had supposed.

As she watched, it moved, swivelling to face her. It was not trash, she realised, no shapeless mound, but a human figure, a silhouette outlined against the snow. Lia didn't know if this was an adult or a child, the slight build could have been either. The features were not distinct from here, and there was snow in her eyes. It began to make its way towards her. Then she saw the long gown brushing the snow, powder sticking to the hem. Lia recognised it as the one she'd selected for Miss Codling. Plain brown wool with horn buttons down the front, suitable for a spinster.

"How did she get out here? She can't be here, it doesn't work like that..." The 'grams were part of the building. They didn't go outside for a cigarette break or a breath of air, anymore than would a lightbulb. Lia's breath was white in the gelid air. Miss Codling was not producing breath at all, and nor was her chest moving. You expected that from a 'gram. She was looking directly at Lia. That, you didn't expect, Lia told herself, even as the woman approached her, not gliding, but standing on top of the snow in her button boots. She advanced, unhurried but steady, her arms at her sides, her expression calm. She'd never had an expression of any sort before. They hadn't needed to supply one. There'd never been any light flickering behind those brown eyes. Until now. Lia drew back, struggling against the wind. She didn't want to take her own eyes from the woman's face.

"She's got lovely long eyelashes, we never gave her those, where did they come from? It's the paint in the house, I've breathed something in, some chemical. I understand I'm hallucinating, but I'm on my feet." She found that she was talking aloud, through freezing lips, the skin of which felt puckered and dry. Jane Codling was only feet away, posture straight as a poker, unhindered by the gale. Her sandy hair showed under the edge of a sensible bonnet trimmed with brown ribbon, suitable for a maiden aunt. "She's made of light, she cannot harm me." Jane's own lips crimped into a smile, showing teeth that were not part of her specification, even as Lia's mumbled words were snatched away by the storm. Miss Codling only came up to Lia's shoulder, but right now, that didn't feel like an advantage. Lia stumbled back inside.

As she fell back into the hallway, the icy wind blew through the building, carrying the blizzard with it. Drifts already lay on the windowsills, as though the house had been left roofless for years. She saw that a man in a striped waistcoat and brown fustian breeches was coming down the stairs as though he owned them. She knew him as Samuel Gelatly, yeoman farmer, died 1802, probably of pneumonia. She had dressed him, picked out his wig, set him to walk through the house like a clockwork toy. That seemed like something that had happened long ago, when there was warmth somewhere in the world. She'd never known such cold. They called it being starved with cold, she was starving down to a bundle of frozen sticks, crouched on her knees on the chequered tiles, that were already glazed with frost.

Samuel walked across the hall with the same steady tread as Jane Codling, who had followed her in, and now stood blocking the doorway, arms at her sides, eyes aglitter, mouth curved upwards. Samuel's eyes met Lia's. They were colder than the snow, hard as black ice. Somewhere in the house, another woman's voice began to sing, pure and sweet.

"When we awaken, under the snow..." Other voices, many more voices than there were 'grams, old and young, joined in:

"We bring the winter wherever we go..."

SCARLET HIDE MOLLY

They were three old women who needed passage through the cold mountains. Snow blinded them, cold bit at their bones, and a stranger watched their progress, yet they had marched for three days to reach the white, windy pass, and they had only another two left to their journey.

Nonetheless, they were three old women and they needed rest. They cleared the snow from beneath a great conifer and each set off to gather firewood as night blanketed the mountains.

After an hour, each returned with a bundle of sticks, and the crone whose fingers remained nimble, called Fingers, built a fire with flint and tinder. Soon a roaring blaze told the snow to fall elsewhere and the three old women warmed their hands by the flames. Two ate cold turnips from their packs, while the one whose teeth remained strong, called Teeth, chewed salted jerky, her big mittens wrapped tight around the meat as if the others might take it. The one whose eyes were clear watched the storm swirl around their camp.

Beyond the firelight, a shadow slipped through the snow.

Fingers told the others this was so. Teeth said she had noticed nothing. The last woman, Eyes, said she had seen a shape, and the shape's eyes had seen her. The cold mountains were well-traveled and each woman lived in the region—each knew what lived there.

"Raw Red Mountain Witch," said Fingers.

"Scarlet Hide Molly," said Teeth.

"Skinless She-Devil," said Eyes. "Likely been watching us since we wandered here."

"Keep the fire bright and be willing to fend her off if she gets brave," Fingers said.

"She fears fire?" Teeth asked.

"Perhaps. I can't say for certain. But I know what goes wrong when the witch skulks and the fire burns low." Fingers' forlorn sigh was the kind only a woman can breathe. "When I was a lass and lived on the north side of these mountains with my family, there was a winter when one mountain came crashing down, like it was built of ice and snow, no soil or stone at all. The village was buried, even my home, but we dug paths from house to house, and had food to last until spring melted the mountain away.

"But the Red Witch was on the mountain, and to this day they say she brought the ice and snow down upon us. Through the tunnels, we set fires to keep watch for her. My home had little enough firewood, and one night when my pa was away, we heard her coming through the tunnels, crying of cold and pain. My brother said it was a ghost and couldn't hurt us.

"He was wrong about that and didn't take to keeping the fire lit. When it went out there was screaming and you'd swear another mountain was coming down. I lit up the fire again like my pa taught me, and there my brother sat, a little blood on his face, but no worse for wear. He tells me he fought her off, that raw woman. But then the fire flitted once more, and when I lit it up again, I found hands on me, wearing my brother's skin, only they weren't his hands. You could see her raw nails poking through his fingers, long and sharp and black.

"I shoved her away with a flaming stick, but the fire wouldn't last long. I did the only thing I could think—put my own house to torch. It burned bright and hot enough to melt the snow and let in the sun. That's when we found my dead brother, robbed of his skin, and likely that witch ran off with it. Don't know what she did with it later. Maybe she wore it, pretending she was a strapping lad to lure maidens away from their villages."

"Feh," Eyes said. "You never had a brother that handsome. Not if he looked like you."

Fingers nodded. "This was many years ago. I suppose such a skin shriveled up, even here in the mountains."

"No one's skin lasts long up here," Teeth said, lowering her jerky. "Be it on a live man or a dead woman, it'll turn red, and then black, and it won't be good to anyone. Same was true for Scarlet Hide Molly."

"Said that name before," Eyes said. "My eyes might be best, but my ears are fine as well. She some girl who came up here to die?"

Teeth nodded. "Yes, but not like you think. Molly is your Skinless She-Devil of the mountains." Firelight glowed off the old woman's incisors. "In days past, these mountains weren't always cold and most anyone would have the legs and will to pass through them, even a slip of a girl like Molly. Of course, it wasn't always decent folk who'd come wandering by. Not at all, ladies. Up in the higher peaks, you'd have ruffians, outlaws, and savage men.

"One day, Molly comes through with a song on her lips and flowers in her basket, and she stops to pick a few more. That's when the shadows fall on her,

not three, not ten, but thirteen, and they belong to the worst lot of men you'd ever seen. They want all she has to give, but this Molly comes from tough blood and old stones, so she fights them like a wild cat.

"The men knock her down and say she's dead. They go about taking the few copper coins she had, and there'd be nothing else to get from her, to hear it said by men of the cities. But the mountain men weren't all from cities, ladies. They figure, if her hide isn't good alive, it's good dead. So they take out their knives and cut the skin from her, leaving nothing but a red mess where a girl had been.

"Only this girl isn't dead then, not yet. She chases after the lot, wanting her skin back, and they don't notice since they don't think anyone's around to follow. Up, up, up they climb, up to the mountain peaks to camp. When all goes quiet and dark, Scarlet Hide Molly sneaks in and slits their throats. She's looking for her skin, looking everywhere, and finds it's already dried by the fire. Could only make a vest out of it, if you stretched it thin.

"Some say she dies then, but I say she doesn't. I say she goes around that camp, cutting the men's flesh, learning how to skin them one by one until she can peel it off with nothing but her fingernails. Then she cuts out their bones and breaks them up, so they can't go looking for their own skins. No rest for the wicked, they say, and she won't let them have it. When all the bones are powder, filling up some big bowl, she tosses the stuff over the mountainside and you can't tell bone dust from snowflakes then. Ever since, the mountains have gotten white snow, cold enough so Molly's flesh don't rot, but too cold for her to get a real skin. Those killers' skins kept her raw flesh warm for a while, but ever since she needs new hides to cover herself. Can't leave on account of the cold keeping her going, and can't quit killing or the cold will kill *her*."

"Was your husband a fisherman?" Eyes asked.

"Might be." Teeth shrugged. "Why you say that?"

"Because that sounds like a fishwife's tale. These mountains have been cold all my life."

"How old are you?" Fingers asked.

"Old enough not to answer that," Eyes said. "Never heard the tale either."

"Might be your ears are going after all."

"Not so," said Eyes. "I hear that Skinless She-Devil creeping closer when even I can't see through the dark. *Crunch, crunch,* that's how she goes in the snow." Firelight flickered in the old woman's eyes. "Some men were killed here just last

week, her most recent slaying. Band of sellswords, I hear. They were coming over the mountain one way or the other for one war or another. Had a local guide who warned them not to head through at night, but it was some emergency, or so I've heard."

Eyes lifted a shriveled finger. "Only that boy who was leading them made it out. He came down from the slopes and met a few of those sellswords' friends, told them they were gone, that the witch had them. Those friends spit in his face, told him no woman would get the best of their company, and they went marching into the mountains as well. Not a one came out."

"As it is with Scarlet Hide Molly," Teeth said. "Gone to the cold mountains, and never seen again."

"None of them went home, true," Eyes said. "Didn't say no one saw them again. That guide went back in, maybe looking to get even, maybe looking to get money, but he didn't find payback or pay. Middle of the mountain pass, he looked up during the dawn as the sun was just coming up behind the slopes, and there he saw the black shapes. At first he thought they were flags and banners from the sellswords' camp.

"Then the sun rose little higher and he saw a little better. The sellswords' swords were dug in the snow, and from the hilts flew their hides, a trail of banners belonging to the Skinless She-Devil herself. She's not keeping warm. The skins are her bloody trophies and a warning for all good people to keep clear of the pass."

"So we're not good people then?" Fingers asked.

"Don't live to our age by being good," Teeth said.

"Might not live much past this age," Eyes said. "The shape of her is upon us." She pointed.

Fingers turned to follow the finger and grasped a burning stick from the fire. "You keep back, witch or ghost, or whatever you are. Go bloody the snow around someone else."

"That's right, you shove off," Eyes said, standing. "You're not about to make us your next skinned sacks of meat."

"Too late," a voice croaked from the shadows. A red, skinless hand breached the outermost firelight and a shivering, crimson creature clambered through the snow.

"It's not too late," Fingers said, waving her skinny torch. "I'll burn out both your eyes and that'll be the end of that."

"I just told them what you've been up to most recent and we're not ready to be your bloody banners," Eyes said.

"I'm what she's been up to most recent," the red thing rasped. The creature dragged herself closer to the fire. She was a cringing old woman, missing the skin of her limbs, her body, and her face. Nothing looked all that strong about her but the teeth, pearly white and all present.

Fingers and Eyes turned back from her to Teeth. Teeth swallowed her last bit of jerky and grinned, revealing a glowing set of incisors. She peeled the face from her flesh with long, black nails, released from their mittens.

"I say she lives," the red woman said. "And I say this skin's gone cold already." A clump of snow crashed through the fire then, dousing the place beneath the tree in darkness, and Scarlet Hide Molly pounced on Fingers and Eyes.

No one came down the other side of the mountains that night, and none on the next day. Some told of travelers who had left one side and never arrived on the other. They were seen by one man who spied hides flying from the ends of burnt sticks, but he didn't know their names and spoke only briefly of them when he returned home.

They were three old women whose screams echoed through the cold mountains.

SCARLET HIDE MOLLY

THE COMPANY MAN

Conrad Shelley stood before a roaring audience of colleagues and a few beaming superiors. He took a small bow. The furor of the applause inclined him to take a second, grander than the first. And though this fanfare revolved all around Conrad's work, he could not help but feel like an imposter—a *fake*. His work was, actually, terrible at best. He had even taken secret measures to ensure that his work was even worse in the many strange weeks leading up to this promotion.

Conrad had never been ambitious. He hardly ever completed his work on time, his reports were sloppy and out of order, and he'd been caught napping at his desk more than three times in the past four months. And yet, during that time he could not escape the onslaught of adulation and praise—ostensibly a result of his *brilliant* work.

Naturally suspicious, Conrad lived his life waiting for the other shoe to drop, for someone to announce that his work had been confused with another's. Each week without this punchline, he tested his suspicions (hence his increased attempts at self-sabotage). It did not matter. Each day he arrived to work he was shown only the highest respects. He'd even attracted a small fan-base of office personnel, much to his discomfort. Under such conditions, he could no longer refill his own coffee mug without some obsequious intern rushing in to assist, even offering to make a fresh pot of coffee, should Conrad deem the current pot too cold or otherwise unsuitable. But awkward and strange as this all was, Conrad soon settled into this role, and learned how to enjoy the perks of his unexpected rise to glory.

And now this. The big day. The day his direct superior had long groomed him for.

The express visit to *The Top*.

Both literally and figuratively, this ritual required that Conrad—with the assistance of building security—ride the elevator up to the highest floor in the building, where he would meet his brand new life. A life of mythical benefits and wild opportunities. A life in which men interacted with gods, and, with a little guidance, soon evolved to become gods themselves. The only position better than "company man" being, of course, "company god."

Conrad's entire office formed a human tunnel. With arms upraised in two rows, the tunnel terminated at the elevator doors. Someone had turned up the music—obnoxious electro-pop.

His prime supervisor, Dalen—a plump bald man in a rumpled pink shirt, clapped directly in Conrad's face, smiling, and cheering for him to venture forth through the eager tunnel of arms. It was like some mystic portal, its walls lined in tapestries of business-casual attire. Shamus Grandy, a high-ranking employee with a handlebar mustache and a cheap hairpiece, gave Conrad a painful slap on the back. Hunched and spry, Conrad gamboled his way through his soon-to-be-former colleagues, and arrived at the elevator.

One thing led to another. Conrad watched the doors close on the exuberant sendoff. The elevator car jerked into motion.

Conrad stood between two large men in body armor, their faces locked straight ahead in icy stares, arms crossed over their massive chests. Between these two titans, Conrad appeared quite small. The long ride upwards felt all the longer, thanks to the accompaniment of lonesome Muzak.

When the doors reopened, Conrad crumpled to his knees. Beyond the elevator car, a cold, vast darkness awaited. Feeling weak, Conrad had to be lifted upright and dragged forth by the two giants in body armor.

Barely comprehending his sur-roundings, only one thing seemed clear to Conrad Shelley: he had somehow arrived at the brink of outer space. Or, rather, a penthouse on the cliffs of the cosmic beyond. From this well-furnished room, with its granite floors and ambient lights, Conrad met a vista of stars and nebulae, laid bare and churning in the black of space. There was no glass barrier between himself and the infinite, the entire room was open to the ghostly howling of solar winds.

In the near distance, a staircase led up to a stone pillar that overlooked the drop off. From the top of this pillar one could lean out and watch fiery comets sail down through blinking blackness, like matches tossed into the dark. This pillar was already occupied by two figures, engaged in what would come to be a last farewell. One—a hairy little fellow—stood dressed in business-casual attire, the other wore a hooded robe of silky maroon. In the arms of the guards, Conrad watched in mute horror as the red-robed figure made a priestly gesture and then took hold of the other's shoulders.

The hairy little fellow was now led forth to the edge of the pillar. A black beard and a bowl cut, the hairy little fellow wore short-sleeves and a clip-on tie. Weeping, he turned his face to make a parting inquiry, but was too late. One push from the red-robed figure and the little man went toppling out into the frosty dark of deep space.

And it wasn't true; what they said about no one being able to hear a scream in space. Conrad heard it. He heard it, until he didn't hear it. And then it was done.

Not missing a beat, the two security guards redoubled their grip on Conrad's arms and started hauling him up to the pillar. The red-robed figure turned from the edge of space and gestured them onward and upward, only a mask of shadow beneath its hood.

Conrad felt it at last. The other shoe had dropped. Horrific as it was, he couldn't help but feel some small sparkle of relief.

It all happened in a messy and clumsy silence at the top of the world.

After much struggle and relent, Conrad somehow finally managed, like a fox in eel-skin, to slip free of his captors. Conrad ran this way and that. The guards gave chase. The red-robed figure looked on from the pillar, waving its arms. At last, Conrad slipped inside the open elevator car. The metal doors slid shut on two snarling brute faces in murderous pursuit.

The bell chimed. The Muzak resumed. Conrad rode the elevator down to the ground floor; he felt nervous, wondering how it would be when he returned to his former office, after his brief visit to The Top.

When the doors opened and the bell chimed, Conrad stumbled out on high alert. Much to his surprise however, his caution proved unnecessary. Hunched at their computers, the workers appeared totally indifferent to the frantic escape of their former hero, Conrad Shelley. His egress from the building was casual—almost disappointingly so, Conrad thought. He unlocked his ancient station wagon, parked in one of the reserved spaces that he'd had the pleasure of calling his own for these past three months.

He drove home. No one seemed to follow. He began to feel the onset of some type of fevered sickness.

Upon returning home he was immediately rushed into bed by the landlady. She took his temperature and yelped. He was in a bad way. High fever. His skin pallid, fingers trembling at the sheets. She felt certain that his brains would melt if she didn't stay with him, holding the ice to his forehead. As he drifted off to sleep, Conrad muttered of wild conspiracies and deep space. Dabbing a compress of ice cubes and terrycloth across his burning brow, the landlady paid these febrile rantings no mind whatsoever, chalking it up to the ordinary work-related stresses of a dedicated company man.

She nursed Conrad back to health for the next week and a half. When, finally, the convalescent came to, and could sustain cognizance for more than a few minutes, the landlady informed him that the company had called many times throughout the preceding days and nights. They wanted to wish Conrad a speedy recovery. She also informed Conrad that Dalen had called that very morning to say that, due to the unfortunate timing of his fever, Conrad was being granted a month's paid vacation, starting that same day. She also made sure to remember, in her retelling, that Dalen had stressed how this generous hiatus from work would not cut into the several vacation days that Conrad had earned over the past year.

"Now isn't that something," the landlady said, rising from her chair to empty the bedpan.

Conrad lay in bed, in the cramped darkness of his apartment, and listened to the cheerful humming and splashing that issued from the lighted crack in the bathroom door. Although weakened, Conrad found all of his faculties were now focused on the company, especially its practice of jettisoning employees into deep space.

A week passed. He began to feel stronger. And though the nightmares persisted, Conrad was up and moving around again, eating solid foods, and planning his return to work.

A sunny afternoon, dead leaves in the road, Conrad's blue station wagon came to a stop at the curb. Across the street was the work campus parking lot. In the center of the lawn, surrounded by trim landscaping and impressive statuary, loomed the building where he had worked for as long as he could remember. Even in the light of day, the building possessed a quality of menace. With just three days left of his impromptu vacation, Conrad wanted to be prepared, mentally and emotionally for his return to work. This was a reconnaissance mission.

Sweating, Conrad realized that it would take a great amount of fortitude to go through with the return. From his car, Conrad could see the parking lot for low-level employees. It would be lunchtime soon, and Conrad planned to eat at the appointed company time.

Conrad chewed on his tuna sandwich and potato chips, now and then sipping hot black coffee, poured fresh from a thermos. Meanwhile, several employees emerged from the building to eat their lunches at the many picnic tables and benches around campus, others went to their cars to get lunch off-site. Watching and eating, Conrad scanned the individuals pouring out onto the walkways and into the parking lot.

He did a double-take. He lowered the thermos lid from his lips and spat a mist of coffee across the windshield.

"How could it be?" Conrad wondered, shaking his head.

"No, that little fellow is an ice cube in space by now, this must be another person entirely—it's that, or my mind is playing dirty tricks!"

In the parking lot across the street, a hairy little fellow ducked into his red hatchback and slammed the door. Conrad quickly put his lunch away and buckled his seatbelt.

Drumming his hands impatiently on the wheel he waited for the red hatchback to putter out onto the road.

Tailing at a safe distance, Conrad followed the red hatchback for a mile and a half. When the ride was over Conrad found himself idling in the parking lot of Kaiser's, a small red and yellow fast food restaurant with a giant, smiling beagle's head for a mascot. A few spaces over, the door of the red hatchback opened and slammed shut. Conrad watched from his idling car, as the hairy little fellow cheerfully kicked dead leaves across the battered asphalt on his way into the restaurant.

Conrad felt certain now that this was the same exact fellow he'd witnessed thrown into space by the red-robed figure a month prior. But he wanted to confirm this by getting a closer look. Fifteen minutes later, Conrad stood beside the window, watching the hairy little fellow eat a hamburger and fries, at a table inside the fast food restaurant. Though he was being watched, the man paid Conrad no mind. And though it might have been a twin, Conrad doubted that.

"No," he thought, "That is the same hairy little fellow alright—not a doubt in my mind. "But then... how? I saw that poor sucker get bumped, ass-over-tea-kettle, out into the stars!"

Conrad was correct. It was the same person, alive and well, and eating poorly. As casual a dead man as one could ever hope to see.

"But then, how could he be dead?" Conrad asked himself, screwing up his eyes. He believed there were limits and natural laws of possibility that could not be defied. And here, now, that hairy little anomaly, enjoying a hamburger and French fries behind a wall of filthy, smudged glass. In broad daylight, no less! It was too much for Conrad to bear. He gave up and plodded back to his blue station wagon.

He started home. However (as if one anomaly weren't enough), Conrad found himself suddenly returned to the curb out in front of his work building. He

didn't know what he was looking for now. And yet he was there, staked out.

He remained in position well after the red hatchback bumped its way back into the parking lot. He'd watched the hairy little fellow wind his way up the path, dusting crumbs off his shirtfront. It was quiet after that. Conrad poured himself some more coffee and rolled down the window. A few dead leaves scuttled across the road, as the sunset glinted fiery in the windows of the tall, dark building.

💾

Ten minutes before closing time, Conrad got out of his station wagon and started across the street. He roamed the parking lot, compelled by some strange whim to visit his reserved parking space.

When he arrived at the space he began to stammer. "No, no, it can't be!" he said. There, in his space, a blue station wagon, identical in every way to the one he'd just left at the curb. First the hairy little fellow, and now a precise replica of his own car in the reserved spot where he'd once parked. How much more could one man take? At the sound of distant voices growing louder, Conrad turned to see a gaggle of colleagues exiting the front doors of the building.

28

THE COMPANY MAN

Like a frightened child, Conrad let his instincts deliver his body to a hiding place, awkwardly crouched behind a small row of green shrubs. These waist-high shrubs ran the length of the parking lot, helping to further segregate the reserved spaces from the rabble. And it was from his humiliating vantage point, beneath the shrubs, that the hidden Conrad Shelley watched—in mental explosions of disbelief—as *Conrad Shelley* came strolling down the walkway with a briefcase in his hand.

Belligerently confident and jocular, this second Conrad was laughing and flirting with an attractive red-headed woman in a well-fitting skirt and blazer, as he walked the pathway toward *his* blue station wagon. The red-haired woman giggled and hung on the imposter's every word. Meanwhile, the hidden Conrad began to twitch and blink his eyes. Try though he might to dispel these evil visions, every time he opened his eyes the second Conrad remained. He and the woman were drawing closer and closer to the shrubs.

Suddenly, Conrad felt a heavy hand clamp down upon his shoulder. He craned his neck to find the security guards from whom he'd previously escaped now looming over him once more. The first held onto him with a death-grip, the other smirked, revealing a brief glimpse

of fangs.

Immediately Conrad made to escape. His efforts were curtailed by the sizzle-snap of a stun-gun, pressed deeply into his ribcage. He fainted straight away and sunk beneath the shrubs, like a limp dummy.

"Hold it right there, Mister Shelly," the second guard called over the shrub.

"We've got a situation here, folks," the first guard said. "Dangerous intruder. Please stay where you are."

The second Conrad and the red-headed woman stopped in their tracks.

"Come on," she said, pulling at the second Conrad's arm. "Let's take my car. I'll drop you off later."

The second Conrad smiled lasciviously.

"Later as in tonight, or tomorrow morning?"

The woman blushed.

"Oh, Conrad. You're so bad!"

"That's not what I've heard."

The woman laughed like a bird. He winked and wrapped his arm around her back. They turned and started off in another direction.

As they strolled away, the second Conrad raised his briefcase and coolly pointed a finger to the guards, signaling his appreciation for their hard work. The guards waved back, looking pleased and eager to be of service, proud to be the sworn protectors of good company folks. Yes, it was a thing to be proud of, indeed. The guards waited for the two employees to be out of sight, before they turned to the task at hand. Reaching down, they lifted the prostrate body.

When Conrad finally awoke, he was back at *The Top*, a cold solar wind sweeping in from a network of deathless constellations.

JAMES DORR

HOLLY JOLLY

**Have a holly, jolly Christmas!
It's the best time of the year.**

— Johnny Marks

He hated *Star Trek*. But what could he do? By an accident of fate, warriors of the Gl'iel—thin and with ears that came to points at their upper tips—resembled a popular character on a TV show on this backwater planet. A science fiction series that seemed to be constantly rerun on something called the "Syfy Channel." And so, while the enlisted ranks suffered ear-bobs and the consequent dulling of their special Gl'iel senses (thus passing themselves off as high-school age humans), officers like Chu'ka were forced to find other means to blend in with the Earthling population.

It wouldn't do to pass this planet up—too many species as it was were forced to compete for so few globes suitable for expansion. But fortunately there were *Star Trek* conventions on nearly every weekend in this sector, where Chu'ka not only looked like he belonged, but was in a position to learn Earthling secrets. He was always welcome at parties as long as he wore his "uniform," an insultingly bland parody of actual Gl'iel military regalia. He would imbibe tongue-loosening liquids and chat about other "cons" he had attended. His hosts, in turn, would blabber about their lives, their mates, and—of special interest to Chu'ka—their jobs. On one occasion, he learned of an upcoming Earth-wide ceremony that could be used to his advantage.

At least he could get rid of his *Star Trek* disguise, although, he had to admit it had served him well thus far. "Going to an audition," he had learned to say on those occasions when he was challenged between conventions, "and I haven't had time to get out of costume." The line had gained him the sympathy and even the respect of the planet's local authorities.

Indeed, sometimes these people, ostensibly guards to *catch* enemies like him, were downright nice. "A pity they'll be killed," he often said to himself. But business was business ––and his was conquering this planet, that, as he had learned, was on the verge of a celebration of something called Christmas.

He had learned well the details of this "Christmas" season at subsequent parties that he had attended, the celebration itself as well as the weeks that led up to it. It was easy for him to infiltrate one of Earth's largest stores, in one of the planet's most important cities—a place called New York—under a new guise of "Holly Jolly, the Santa-Land Elf." And with a new uniform to boot, one of bright greens and red and white stripes, of pom-poms and tassels.

This was a uniform almost befitting the dignity of a Gl'iel commander!

Once he was established in his new position—photographing the children that flocked to sit on the lap of the fat one called "Santa"—he used his ear-points to telepathically contact the other Gl'iel officers who had taken similar posts in other department stores and malls throughout the planet. From there they signaled their enlisted minions to gather, their weapons disguised as newly-bought toy ray guns, glistening with plastic and buzzing with battery-powered lights and noise-makers.

For this was the night, the night of nights, when Chu'ka himself would begin the carnage. He had discovered that one of Earth's customs was that on this night they called Christmas Eve, the planet's largest TV stations traditionally aired something called a "news special," a segment of which would be at this very place. What happened here would be seen all over the land. The Earthlings themselves would transmit his attack signal. He waited as camera and light crews converged on the overweight, scarlet-clad Santa. Converged on him and the others, the elves and pixies of the Christmas Village displacing the humans once in these positions. Converged on the gangly "schoolchildren" who pressed about, slack-jawed in anticipation, "toys" clutched in their arms.

Then, seeing the camera lights flash to red, Chu'ka raised his own candy-cane-disguised blaster when, suddenly, the "Santa" rose up. Fur-trimmed shreds of cloth flew about, revealing the armor of a supreme fighting chief of the Gl'iel's hated rivals, the Blorb'b. The creature's tentacles, hidden beneath folds of belly flab, slapped Chu'ka's puny weapon aside, before reaching into its gift-sack of death to retrieve even deadlier arms. Other Santas across the land, in stores and on street corners, revealed themselves as well.

It was for Chu'ka, as well as for Earth, decidedly *not* the best time of the year.

Greetings Intrepid Wanderer of the Cosmos! We've come to your planet to discuss a matter of immense galactic import: you're being **INVADED**! The looming specter of Planet Scumm approaches your orbit and there is only one way to fend off the imenent, hostile alien invasion...

SUBSCRIPTIONS

Stories composed from the most supple asteroids and precious moon rocks!

Not buying would imply you're some kind of dummy. You're not a dummy, are you?

Guaranteed to make you ooze every time!

Be the first in your quadrant to receive a copy!!

ARE YOU TIRED OF REFRESHING OUR STORE PAGE LIKE SOME KIND OF **JUNKIE GERBIL** IN A MORBID ALIEN SCIENCE EXPERIMENT?

ARE YOU **DREARY AND LONGING** FOR THE LATEST ISSUE, WISHING YOU KNEW WHEN YOUR NEXT TASTE WOULD COME?

DO YOU **HATE** HAVING TO FOLLOW US ON TWITTER?

JUST SUBSCRIBE, DUMMY!

GET ALL THE UPDATES YOUR HEART DESIRES AT **PLANETSCUMM.SPACE**

CPSIA information can be obtained
at www.ICGtesting.com
Printed in the USA
LVHW020805130819
627419LV00006B/53/P